The Dragon Painter

Retold by
Rosie Dickins

Illustrated by
John Nez

Reading Consultant: Alison Kelly
Roehampton University

Everyone loved Chang's
pictures. People came from
all over China to see them.

3

Chang painted
misty mountains.

Splish Splosh Splish

He painted
vases full of flowers.

But his animal pictures were best of all.

Splish

Splosh

His butterflies and birds really seemed alive.

Splash!

And you could almost see
his rabbits twitch their noses.

One day, Chang saw the
village priest at the temple.

The priest was upset.
"Look at that statue," he
said sadly.

It's so dirty.

Two pigeons had built a
nest in the roof, right above
the statue.

10

Chang went to find his
paints and a ladder.

Splish

Be careful!

He climbed up to the
roof and painted a
fierce eagle.

13

He gave it long, long claws and a sharp, sharp beak.

Splosh

The pigeons were terrified.
They squawked. They
flapped. They flew away...
and never came back.

15

Chang's pictures became famous. One day, the Emperor of China heard about them.

His animal pictures are the best in China.

Now, the Emperor needed someone to paint his new temple. "I shall ask Chang," he decided.

Chang planned a splendid picture. It had four dragons...

one...

two...

three...

four...

...one for each wall.

To the
temple →

A huge crowd gathered
at the temple to watch
Chang paint.

On the first wall, Chang drew a pearl-white dragon. The dragon breathed out clouds of steam.

Splish

It looked perfect, except for one thing. The dragon had no eyes.

The second dragon was
jade-green. This one had
bushy eyebrows and a big,
spiky nose.

Splosh

His face looks funny.

But the green dragon's
eyes were empty too.

23

On the third wall, Chang painted a huge gold dragon. He gave it a long, coiled tail, curling around its body.

Splish

The gold dragon didn't
have any eyes either.

The last dragon had gleaming red scales and wicked claws.

He's scary!

Splosh!

But, just like the
others, the red dragon's
eyes were empty.

Chang turned to the
Emperor and bowed. "Do
you like the dragons, my
lord?" he asked.

"I do," the Emperor replied.
"There's just one problem."

"I can't paint their eyes," said Chang. "Dragons are magical creatures...

...if I paint their eyes, they will come to life."

Live dragons are dangerous!

The Emperor didn't
believe Chang. He thought
the painter was teasing him.

Stuff and
nonsense!

"Don't be silly," he snapped. "I order you to finish these dragons!"

"I can't!" cried Chang.
But it was no good. He had
to obey the Emperor. With a
wobbly hand, he painted
eyes on the first dragon.

-sp-sp-splish-

BOOM!

What's that noise?

There was a rumble of thunder and the sky grew dark.

35

Chang paused. He was worried.

"What are you waiting for?" the Emperor grumbled. "Get on with it!"

So Chang turned and
dotted in the eyes of the
jade dragon...

the gold dragon...

and the red dragon.

Chang finished and...

CRACK!

...a bolt of lightning split
open the temple roof.

The jade dragon blinked
and raised its head.

Wh-what's happening?

Its spiky nose cracked
one of the temple columns.

Then the pearl dragon
yawned, showing rows of
sharp, white teeth.

It breathed out clouds of
burning steam. The people
nearby ran for their lives.

41

Suddenly, both dragons
jumped from their walls
and flew through the hole
in the roof.

They flew higher
and higher, until they
disappeared into the clouds.

The red and gold dragons began to stir. Quickly, Chang grabbed his brush. He painted heavy chains around their necks.

"Splish"

"Splosh"

The dragons rattled their
chains, but they couldn't
fly away.

45

So, the Emperor had to make do with only two dragons on his temple walls.

He can't say I didn't warn him!

But they were the
best painted dragons in
all of China.

The Dragon Painter is a traditional Chinese story.
People have been telling it for over a thousand
years. Even today, people in China say "painting
the dragon's eyes" to describe the finishing touches
which bring a work of art to life.

Series editor: Lesley Sims
Designed by Russell Punter and Louise Flutter
Chinese story advisor: Evelyn Ong

First published in 2006 by Usborne Publishing Ltd., Usborne House,
83-85 Saffron Hill, London EC1N 8RT, England. www.usborne.com
Copyright © 2006 Usborne Publishing Ltd.
Illustrations Copyright © John Nez 2006. The right of John Nez to be
identified as the Illustrator of this Work has been asserted by him in
accordance with the Copyright Designs and Patents Act 1988.